Grandpa's ~~G~~
Sall~~y~~

Viking Kestrel

Sam looks inside the shed. What a lot of flowerpots – ooh, what's that?

Now they help Grandpa to plant some seeds. Polly waters them to make them grow.

Grandpa's tied a swing to a branch of the old apple tree.

How many goldfish are there in the pond?

Grandpa gives Sam and Polly a ride in the wheelbarrow to see the bunnies.

Time for tea. Mmm! Granny's home-made biscuits are delicious.